# Flurry the Bear

and

## The Christmas Wish

J.S. Skye

Edited by Jane Inman
jane.inman@comcast.net

Cover illustrations by Manuela Soriani.
manuelasoriani@gmail.com
donanza.me/Manuela_Soriani

Covers digitally painted by Alvin Hew.
www.AlvinHew.com

Characters drawn by Wes Talbott.
wes-talbott.deviantart.com

Characters colored by Lorna Brighton.
kiwiboob.deviantart.com

ISBN: 0615688853
ISBN-13: 978-0615688855

# DEDICATION

This book is dedicated to everyone that longs to find good clean entertainment. Flurry the Bear is meant to be exactly that, something for all to enjoy and to be a form of entertainment that's innocent and safe for all ages to experience. It's my hope that Flurry will be a blessing to everyone and that he'll bring happiness, joy, and laughter to every life he touches.

# CONTENTS

Acknowledgments  i

1  A Mother's Joy    1

2  Misunderstood    26

3  Mr. Kringle    54

4  The Toy Factory    74

5  Toy Store Chase    99

6  A Lesson to Learn    118

7  Flurry's New Life    133

# ACKNOWLEDGMENTS

I would like to thank God for inspiring me
and giving me the ability to be creative. It
has enabled me to imagine and write about
the world of Flurry the Bear and beyond. I'd
also like to thank my loving wife, who has
been such a supportive person in my life.
With her by my side, I feel like I can do
anything. I'd like to thank all of the people
that have influenced me and encouraged me
to move forward with my writing projects. If
I were to make a list of people that have
helped me it could potentially be as long as
my arm. The long and short of it is that many
people have encouraged me to write as well
as giving me ideas and inspiration along the
way. I'm also very thankful for all the people
that assisted me in the editing process. I'm
very grateful to all of you and I'll always
remember what you've done for me.

# Chapter 1
## A MOTHER'S JOY

Once upon a time, there was a cozy, quaint little village in the cold, blustering land of the North Pole. This village was home to a community of teddy bears. Among the houses of these fuzzy neighbors was a cream colored house with a brown roof and a blue front door. Behind the windows, blue curtains could be seen, matching the front door's color. It was a warm, comfortable little house with a chimney to battle the blistering temperatures of this frozen, icy land. In this house lived a lovely teddy bear couple known to everyone as the Snow family.

The Snow family was well loved by the other teddy bears, and they were a very cute couple too. Mr. Snow was of a light brown color, almost the color of golden caramel. In contrast to his light brown fur, he wore a tiny blue bowtie with two little white snowflakes on it. These snowflakes were the Snow family's crest. All members of the Snow family have these very same snowflakes on pieces of their clothing. In fact, each of the teddy bears wore their own family crest on their attire somewhere so they could easily recognize each other. Mr. Snow often wore his utility belt as well, just as if it were one of his garments. He would do this even on his off days. He always said, "You never know when this might come in handy." Mr. Snow was renowned for his expert carpentry skills.

His wife, Mrs. Snow, had fur as white as snow – how fitting that her family name would be Snow! She wore a blue dress with pink hearts at the fringe, and a blue bow adorned the top of her head. The pink hearts matched her pink little nose, making her look all the more adorable. Mr. and Mrs. Snow were a young couple, and they were very happy together. They had been married for many years, but they hadn't yet had any teddy bear cubs of their own.

It's not that Mr. and Mrs. Snow didn't want a teddy bear cub to call their own, but Mrs. Snow assumed that it would be too much to ask such a large favor of Christopher Kringle. After all, Christopher was the one who granted life to all of the teddy bears, with the help of the one that gave Christopher this ability to work miracles. Without him, it would be impossible for a teddy bear to come to life.

Every Christmas Eve, Christopher Kringle would grant a wish to one lucky citizen of the teddy bear village. He would make his choice by putting all of their names into his big glass globe at the center of town, and he would reach in and draw a name at random. The name-drawing would take place on the morning of Christmas Eve, so that the teddy bears would have time to plan what they would ask of Christopher later that night. At midnight on Christmas Eve, all of the teddy bears would gather at the town center and celebrate the granting of one wish before Christopher went out to make his rounds. Up until now, neither Mr. nor Mrs. Snow had ever been chosen, but this Christmas Eve things would be different.

It was the morning of Christmas Eve, and it seemed like any other day. Mr. Snow was heading off to work, and Mrs. Snow made him a sack lunch to take with him. Mr. Snow was on his way out the door, almost forgetting his lunch. It was an easy thing to forget on a day like this. Christmas Eve is always an exciting time, and Mr. Snow, being a carpenter, had a lot of work to do. He found considerable joy in knowing that his creations would be loved by children all over the world. Mrs. Snow chased after her husband, calling out to him, "Honey! You forgot your lunch."

"Why thank you, my dear. What would I do without you?" Mr. Snow replied.

Mrs. Snow gave him a kiss on the cheek as she handed him the sack lunch she had prepared for him. "Goodbye. Have a good day. I love you!" She waved goodbye.

With a big smile on his face, Mr. Snow waved back saying, "I love you, too!"

Mrs. Snow returned to the house and shut the door behind her. Looking out from the window, she could see the small, distant shape of her husband, off in the distance, as he walked to work. Turning her back to the window, she decided to do some house cleaning. She had planned to have guests over for the evening and wanted the house to look presentable.

Mrs. Snow hadn't been cleaning for more than a few minutes when there was a knock at the door. "That's odd," she said, "I'm not expecting anyone this early." She gracefully skipped over to the door, anxious to see who it might be. Peeking through the window, she could see her brother-in-law's wife, Bubbles, standing outside. Bubbles was a youthful teddy bear, despite her age – well, at least youthful at heart, and that's what matters. She always had a way with children due to her cheerful personality. Mrs. Snow opened the door to see an excited look on Bubbles' face. Her yellow fur made her look even more radiant.

Bubbles rushed into the house and gave Mrs. Snow a big teddy bear hug. Surprised, Mrs. Snow asked, "Wow! What's that for?"

Equally surprised, Bubbles replied, "You don't know? Haven't you heard the news? You were chosen in the lottery this morning. You're going to get to make a wish tonight. It's so exciting!"

Mrs. Snow didn't reply. In fact, she didn't know what to say. It was like a dream and she was afraid that someone might wake her up at any moment. She stood still, as if she were a statue. A tear trickled down her cheek.

Bubbles continued on, "This is great! Now you can finally have your own teddy bear cub. I'll be an aunt! Then your cub and my cubs can play together and …"

Before Bubbles could finish, Mrs. Snow realized that she had a very limited amount of time before she would need to make her wish. Almost in a panic she stopped Bubbles mid-sentence, "Oh my! I have to go! I need to make preparations!"

Before Bubbles could even reply, Mrs. Snow had already bolted out the door. Realizing this, Mrs. Snow turned around and ran back to her friend and family member, "I'm so sorry, but I have to go. Thank you for telling me. I'll see you tonight, right?" Mrs. Snow waved goodbye as she ran off again.

The trip to the town center seemed to take but mere moments. Mrs. Snow could think of nothing else but what she had to get done. She rushed into the little shop, out of breath. "Well, hello there," said the storekeeper. He was about a foot taller than Mrs. Snow and he had dark brown fur, a forest green apron, and bifocals.

Still gasping for breath, Mrs. Snow answered him, "Hello. *pant* Do you have white … *pant* … fur that I could purchase from you?"

"Well, let's take a look. I don't see why I wouldn't. I try to keep my shop fully stocked at all times." The storekeeper walked over to a shelf containing stacks of fur. He proceeded to rummage through the different types and colors of fur. "I have brown, green, black, blue, pink, and … Aha! White!" he said, pleased to have found it.

"Oh thank you so much!" Mrs. Snow replied in a broken voice, as she was, once again, nearing tears of joy. "How much do I owe you?"

"Well, your husband is a good friend and since it's Christmas Eve, consider it a Christmas gift. I can see how much it means to you, and your joy is enough of a payment to me."

For a second time this morning, Mrs. Snow was without words. "I don't know what to say. Thank you so much! If there's anything I can do for you …"

"You already have," the storekeeper replied as he smiled and walked back to the counter.

"Thank you again, I won't ever forget this." Mrs. Snow rushed out the door, almost tripping at the threshold, and hurried home.

The day came and went in a pinch, and Mrs. Snow now found evening fast approaching. Mr. Snow was just coming home. As he opened the door, he noticed that the house hadn't been cleaned up, as planned. It wasn't common for Mrs. Snow to not be prepared for company. Mr. Snow looked to his left, and over by the fireplace he saw something he didn't expect to see. Sitting on their strawberry-colored couch was Mrs. Snow holding a little ball of white fur. With the fireplace lit, a cup of tea on the coffee table, and Mrs. Snow leaning against the arm of the couch, it was clear to him that she had been hard at work on what he found in her arms.

Mr. Snow quickly approached the side of the couch, eager to see what his wife held in her arms. Wrapped in a blue blanket was an adorable little teddy bear cub. The cub had deep black eyes, a brown nose, and fur whiter than snow. Mr. Snow could see a resemblance to his wife in the little cub. At Mrs. Snow's feet sat a partially finished blue scarf that she was in the process of knitting for her little cub.

Looking down at such a darling teddy bear cub, Mr. Snow said, "He's quite adorable. He has your fur."

"He has your eyes," replied his wife.

"What should we name him?" Mr. Snow asked, as he put his arms around his wife and reached out with one paw to pull the blanket away from the cub's face.

"Well, I was thinking of naming him Flurry. His fur is certainly as white, if not whiter than snow. He is also little, like a little snowflake. What do you think?"

Mr. Snow noticed the sparkle in her eyes. He nodded in agreement and said, "Flurry it is! That's a fine name for my firstborn son." Mr. Snow bent down and gave each of them a kiss on the cheek. "Well, I'll go prepare for the gathering."

"Okay. I'll finish up his scarf and then get prepared too," Mrs. Snow added.

Mrs. Snow had just finished putting the scarf on her little Flurry when a look of horror came across her face. She just realized that she had somehow forgotten something very important. She gently placed her cub in a basket on the couch and quickly ran toward the door. She almost flew out of the doorway, forgetting to grab a coat, close the door, or even inform her husband where she was going. She ran and ran as fast as her little legs would take her. She was traveling the same route she had taken that morning, but for some reason the trip seemed to drag on for what she would've described as an eternity.

Just like before, she arrived at the little shop, out of breath and panting for air. The sign on the door said "Closed." Mrs. Snow fell to her knees and began to cry. The storekeeper was inside cleaning up for the night. He was about to turn out the lights when he heard a strange sound coming from the door. He listened closely and recognized the sound as the mournful weeping of another bear. He opened the door to find Mrs. Snow on her knees in the middle of what would've been a puddle of water had it not become a puddle of ice instead.

"Oh dear! How long have you been out here?" The storekeeper asked.

"I don't know," she sobbed.

"Well, whatever is the matter?"

"I ran out of fur to finish my son, and it's only a few hours till midnight."

"Well, don't give up yet. Let's take a look at what I have. Here, come in out of the cold." The storekeeper held the door for her as he waved her indoors. He grabbed a blanket for her, "Here, this should help warm you up a bit while I help you look."

The storekeeper dug around and checked every shelf, cabinet, and drawer. "Hmmmm … I don't seem to have any more white fur. I have an off-white color you could use. Would that be okay?"

Mrs. Snow shook her head in disbelief.

"I'll be putting in an order for some more. It should be here in about a week."

Mrs. Snow broke down again. Her tears ran down her ivory fur as she planted her face in her paws. "You don't understand, I need it tonight or my son won't be completed in time for the gathering."

"There, there, it's not the end of the world. Ask Mr. Kringle. I'm sure he can make some sort of allowance for you." The storekeeper tried to console her as he rubbed her back.

"It's okay. I should go now. Thank you for the blanket and for trying to help me. Merry Christmas." After returning the blanket to the storekeeper, she went back outside and began the journey back home. Only this time her trip was vastly different. Each footstep was heavy and it took every ounce of her strength to move forward. She walked so slowly that it was now very late in the night when she returned home. As she reached the front door, Mr. Snow came running out to her with an extra coat. "Dear, where have you been? I've been so worried about you. Nobody knew where you were. Are you okay?" Mrs. Snow couldn't answer. She just began to cry and sniffle. Mr. Snow brought her inside and sat her down by the fire shortly before bringing her some tissues for her nose and for wiping her tears. "What is it, darling? You can tell me."

In between her sobs she answered him, "I failed. I failed you, I failed myself, and, most importantly, I failed Flurry."

"Now, now, what's gotten into you? Why

do you feel this way?" asked her husband.

Quickly, and in a raised voice, she replied, "Because! Don't you see! It's almost midnight and our son isn't finished! I forgot to give him a tail and the shopkeeper is all out of white fur and …"

Before she could finish her rant, her husband chuckled, rubbed her back, and interjected, "Sweetie! He's perfect just as he is! He doesn't need to have a tail to be our son. You've created the finest and cutest teddy bear the world has ever seen. You should be proud. I'm certainly proud of you, and I'm proud to have little Flurry as my son, tail or no tail."

Mrs. Snow's face lit up, "Really?" she sobbed.

"Of course!" reassured her husband. Mr. Snow then got up, walked over to the little cub, scooped him into his arms, and put the tiny bear into the arms of his soon-to-be mother. "Here! Hold him while I help you with the door. You don't want to be late for your wish, do you?"

A smile then came across her face. She got up and kissed her husband on the cheek and said, "I love you, my big snuggle bear." Mr. Snow closed the door behind them and off they went to see Christopher Kringle.

As they were arriving at the town center, they could see the entire teddy bear village gathered together. Christopher himself was already there and anxiously waiting for them. "I was beginning to think you weren't going to show up," Christopher exclaimed as he chuckled. "And what have we here? Let me see this handsome fellow." Christopher held out his arms while Mrs. Snow put the little cub safely in his grasp. Christopher examined the little cub more closely and then looked back at Mr. and Mrs. Snow. "You know, this is the cutest, most adorable little teddy bear I've ever seen. Mrs. Snow, you've outdone yourself with your craftsmanship. Your work is deserving of the wish you want me to grant."

"How did you know what my wish was? Before I brought my cub to you, I hadn't yet told you." Mrs. Snow was quite surprised that Mr. Kringle would know such a thing.

Christopher stood up and chuckled out loud, "My dear! Everyone knows how much you've wanted your own cub, and tonight I'm going to grant you that very wish. So, tell me, my dear, what may I call this youngster?"

In unison, Mr. and Mrs. Snow both said,

"His name is Flurry."

Christopher could see how proud they were of their new cub. He crouched back down, peered into the eyes of the little cub, and whispered in the little cub's ear, "Flurry! Flurry! Wake up. Your parents are here to see you." The little cub opened his eyes for the first time, took in a breath of air, and said, "san-ta?"

Christopher immediately looked like he had been taken off guard. There was silence. Christopher hadn't expected Flurry to speak so soon, nor did he know the meaning of the word, "san-ta." Perhaps it was some form of baby speech? Christopher cleared his throat and said, "No, my name is Christopher."

Flurry replied, "Santa!" and clutched Christopher around the neck with a loving hug. After some time of trying to hold it back, amusement broke out among the teddy bears. They all began to giggle, and Christopher himself began to chuckle at how adorable this little bear was.

Christopher stood up and held Flurry up into the air above his head for the entire village to see. Everyone cheered. Mrs. Snow began to cry and her husband put his arm around her, though he could barely contain his own excitement.

Still holding Flurry up in the air, Christopher announced, "Behold! I give you Flurry Snow, son of Mr. and Mrs. Snow! May Flurry and his family be ever blessed. May blessings also be upon all who meet Flurry, as I'm certainly blessed to be able to hold such an adorable teddy bear cub tonight."

Christopher walked over to Mr. and Mrs.

Snow, put Flurry into his mother's arms and said, "Flurry, these are your parents. Be good to them for they love you very much." Flurry looked up at them and said, "Mama? Papa? I love you!" They both hugged him as the entire village shouted with joy and cheered.

Christopher then pulled Mr. Snow aside and said, "You know, he's surprisingly smart, more so than usual. He has a rare and special gift. He really catches on quickly. Take good care of him."

"I most certainly will," Mr. Snow proudly replied.

Then Christopher turned to Mrs. Snow and spoke softly in her ear, "I can see the resemblance to you, but I also noticed he has an uncanny resemblance to the statue. I assume this isn't a coincidence?"

The statue Christopher referred to was of a

hero that had saved the teddy bear village many generations ago. Mrs. Snow answered him and said, "Yes, a little bit. He was certainly an inspiration and I hope my son will follow in the footsteps of greatness."

"Indeed he will. I can foresee it." Christopher spoke confidently.

The bands began to play cheerful music, confetti fell from the sky, and the teddy bears began to dance and celebrate at the center of town. In the commotion of the celebration, Mr. and Mrs. Snow lost sight of Christopher. The last thing they remembered was Christopher saying, "Well, I'm off. I can't delay too long or the children won't be getting their gifts this year," as he chuckled to himself.

Wherever Christopher disappeared to, Mr. and Mrs. Snow didn't know. They were too focused on their newborn son to notice anything else. They were so immeasurably happy that their dreams had finally been realized as they looked down at the shiny little eyes looking back up at them. They finally got their wish. They now had a son.

# Chapter 2
## MISUNDERSTOOD

The sheer joy and excitement Mr. and Mrs. Snow felt was immeasurable. They spent every available minute with their son. As often as time would allow, they took Flurry out to build snowbears, to compete in snowball fights, and to go sledding down the steep hills around the village. Flurry loved to play and everywhere he went, he spread cheer.

It's difficult to know how much time

passed while at the North Pole. Since teddy bears don't age the way real bears do, Flurry always remained the young age of a three-year-old. However, the amount of time passing isn't important. What's important is how Flurry was raised to become what he was destined to be.

As time proved, Flurry was a pretty good bear. However, he would manage to get himself into trouble, every now and then. He would often go to Mrs. Daybear's house to get his buddy, Sunny, and go on adventures, exploring their backyards. You'd be surprised at what secrets are waiting to be discovered in your own backyard.

At the schoolhouse, Flurry would often get talked into sneaking off with Sunny to play. It wasn't done out of defiance to authority or mischief; he was just a child after all, and he was easily influenced by the promise of fun and adventure. Besides, what child wouldn't be lured by the promise of fun and adventure?

One such day, Flurry was staring out the window, watching the snow fall lightly on the tree branches. The sun shone brightly and cast a warmth on his face as he sat at his desk, unaware of anything the teacher was saying to him. Through his fantasies of great adventures that beckoned to him from the distant horizon, a voice began to break through, as if from another world. "Flurry," sounded the voice of his school teacher. But Flurry was in a happy place and didn't hear his name being called. "Flurry." She called out again. "Flurry!" The instructor bellowed.

Flurry jumped with a start and answered, "I didn't do it!"

The classroom laughed while Flurry tried to get his bearings straight.

"No, I called on you to answer the question. What starts with the letter T?"

"Toothpaste?" Flurry answered, uneasily, for he was unsure of himself after not knowing what she had been speaking about. The classroom broke into laughter again.

"Flurry! Were you paying attention at all? Toothpaste isn't a name of an animal." The teacher shook her head as she came and stood over Flurry's desk, pushing back her bifocals.

"It could be! Well, if someone had a pet and named it Toothpaste." Flurry looked up and grinned uneasily as his cheeks began to blush. If Flurry could've made a halo appear above his head, he would have.

The instructor, in her green dress, walked

up to Flurry's desk and stood there glaring at him with disapproval.

Flurry looked up at the gray fur standing at his desk and he began to tear up. "I'm sorry," Flurry cried.

"Sorry isn't good enough. You need to start paying attention. I'm trying to teach the alphabet, and you are off in your own little world. Maybe I should write a letter to your parents?"

"Which letter?" Flurry asked. "You have twenty-six of them to choose from." Flurry misunderstood her meaning, but his statement came across as sarcasm.

"Oh! I see how it is. You want to be a wise guy, eh? So be it! I'll write an extensive letter to your parents and inform them of what a poor student you've been." The instructor huffed as if she were a steam engine, about to let off steam. She quickly spun around, and marched toward her desk at the front of the classroom.

"Oh no! Please don't! I'll do anything! I'll pay attention from now on, I promise!" Before Flurry could get an answer from his teacher, the bell rang.

"You are all dismissed," she informed the class as she continued to walk back to her desk.

Flurry quickly slipped out from his chair and raced toward the door. Flurry had only just escaped when Sunny showed up.

"Hey, Flurry!" Sunny called out to Flurry from down the long hallway.

Flurry waved back at Sunny, "Hello!"

Sunny's yellow fur seemed to brighten Flurry's mood. "Flurry! I thought of something fun we can do."

"What's that?" Flurry replied with excitement.

"There's this amazing tree out in front of our houses. We should climb it and see who can get to the top the quickest."

"I don't know. That sounds fun, but my mama and papa might not like that. They don't think it's safe to climb trees," Flurry replied with a discouraged tone in his voice.

"Come on! Live a little! Nobody will know," Sunny said convincingly as he pulled his red handkerchief up over his face. "See, you can't even tell who I am, can you?"

Flurry wasn't convinced, but he gave in. "Oh, okay. Only for a little bit, and then I need to get home or my mama will be worried about me." Then, a hint of caution crept back in as Flurry asked, "Just promise me we won't climb very high, okay?"

"Sure! I promise." Sunny sounded sincere, so Flurry joined him as they rushed off toward home.

Their choice tree was very close to their homes. They both arrived at the tree and stood still for a few moments contemplating their method of ascending the giant that towered over them. It was clear that getting to the first branch was going to be the biggest challenge. After all, they were only teddy bear cubs, and they weren't very tall. Sunny, after stacking some rocks up, gave Flurry a boost. In return, Flurry pulled Sunny up into the tree with him with the use of his scarf. Flurry's little arms just didn't have the reach he needed.

"I'll race you to the top branch," Sunny challenged.

"Okay," Flurry said in a concerned voice.

He had just taken a peek out from the branches and realized how high up they were. Flurry swallowed hard and closed his eyes as he began the climb.

It's difficult to know how much time passed, but it seemed like mere moments before Flurry and Sunny heard a fur-curling scream. "Sunny! Get down from there this instant! How many times have I told you to stop climbing trees?"

Sunny poked his head out from the branches to find his mother standing at the base of the tree, paws on her hips.

Sunny pulled his head back in, and in a startled voice whispered to Flurry, "It's my mom! I'm in so much trouble! I have to go now. Bye!"

Flurry whispered back, "Okay, goodbye!" He then stuck his head out, to see Sunny's angry mother staring back at him. "Oh! I see what's going on here! This is your fault, isn't it?" she sternly addressed Flurry.

"No it isn't, I promise!" Flurry attempted to defend himself.

"I'll hear no more of it! You're a bad influence on my boy. I don't want you playing with him anymore."

"Mother, Flurry didn't do anything. I asked him to come with me." Sunny attempted to defend Flurry.

Sunny's mother wouldn't have it, "You don't need to make excuses for him. Before you met Flurry, you didn't get in as much trouble as you do now. It's obvious that he has a negative effect on you. It comes from poor upbringing. In the end, it's his parents that are to be blamed. Come on, let's go home." Before she had walked away, she turned back to Flurry, "And you! I have half a mind to have a little chat with your parents too! Maybe they'll finally give you some much needed discipline."

"No, Mrs. Daybear! Please!" Flurry pleaded but his words fell on deaf ears.

Flurry sat in the tree sulking for a while. He wondered why he was so misunderstood by others. How could he be blamed for something that wasn't even his idea? He thought about how he should've just said no. Then, all of a sudden, it dawned on Flurry that his parents would be home soon. Flurry quickly navigated the branches, but his haste didn't prepare him for the patch of ice at the lowest branch. Before Flurry knew what was happening, his foot gave way and he fell from the tree. Luckily, Flurry had two things going for him. First of all, there was a snow drift to cushion his fall. Secondly, he was a teddy bear. Teddy bears don't really have to worry about getting hurt, like a real bear would.

Flurry impacted the snow and a white cloud of fallen snowflakes swirled around him. Flurry got up and brushed off the excess snow, shook his head, and took off running for home.

The distance from the tree to his home wasn't far, but Flurry must have sat up in the tree far longer than he realized. The sun was now beginning to set and to Flurry's horror, Mrs. Daybear was already at the door of his house, speaking with his mother.

Flurry arrived at the door and squeezed in between the door frame and Mrs. Daybear's left leg. Flurry looked back at her from indoors, and was met with the angry scowl on Mrs. Daybear's face. Many of the other bear cubs joked about Mrs. Daybear. They liked to say she permanently had a disgruntled look on her face and that she didn't know how to smile – it's quite ironic, if you consider her family name. Flurry thought about it and realized that he was unable to think of a single moment when Mrs. Daybear didn't look peeved.

"Poor Mrs. Daybear, maybe she just needs a hug," thought Flurry. Before Flurry could dwell on the subject any longer, he was brought back to the moment at hand.

Flurry could hear his mother saying goodbye followed with, "Okay, I'll look into it. Thank you." The door clicked shut and Mrs. Snow turned to face Flurry. Strangely, she didn't appear the way Flurry had anticipated. Instead of looking angry, she looked sad. Tears began to form. "Flurry, I don't know what to say to you right now. Do you know how dangerous that was? What if something bad had happened to you? You're my only son." She began weeping and Flurry felt tremendous guilt. He hadn't thought about how his actions would affect her.

"I'm sorry, Mama." Flurry reassured her with a hug, as he cuddled up against his mother.

Later that evening, Mr. Snow came home to find his wife and son cuddling on the couch. Mrs. Snow, while stroking Flurry's head, looked up at her husband with a concerned look in her eyes. Mr. Snow knew this look well. "What is it?" he asked with hesitation.

"Mrs. Daybear came to see me today. She was angry at Flurry and blamed him for getting her son to climb trees with him." Mrs. Snow relayed the entire story to her husband.

After listening patiently, Flurry's father asked, "Is this true?"

"I did climb a tree with Sunny, but it was his idea. I didn't want to, but ..."

Before Flurry could finish, his father spoke up, "Flurry, what are we going to do with you? You know climbing trees isn't safe, don't you?" he asked him.

"Yes, Papa, I know." Flurry looked down at the floor as he felt regret for making such a foolish decision.

"Then why do you do it?" asked Flurry's father.

"I don't know, maybe because it's fun?" Flurry answered.

That wasn't the answer Flurry's parents wanted to hear. Suddenly, both his mother and father looked angry and stood with their paws on their hips. "Because it's fun? Because it's fun! Go to your room!" shouted Mr. Snow. Tears came down Flurry's soft furry cheeks as he ran to his room.

Mr. Snow sat down in his chair. The look on his face conveyed deep reflection, as he thought about what he should do to properly discipline his son. "What are we going to do with him?" Mr. Snow asked, as he looked at his wife, who was now in tears again.

Standing next to the chair, Mrs. Snow answered, "I'm not sure. Scolding him doesn't seem to work. Maybe we should ground him and forbid him to be able to go outside until he can learn to obey his parents," Mrs. Snow answered, as she rubbed her husband's arm to comfort him. She hoped that it would reassure him that her idea would work. It broke her heart to see Flurry having such a hard time. Seeing Flurry cry is enough to melt the hardest of hearts.

"Well, you know that I work during the day. Will you be able to keep your eye on him all day long?"

Mrs. Snow reassured her husband, "I'm sure I'll be fine." Then in a joking manner she said, "I have eyes in the back of my head."

The next day came. Flurry sat at the front window and watched the other teddy bears having fun outside in the snow. "I'm so bored!" he thought to himself. Flurry hopped down from the windowsill and grabbed his ball and began bouncing it around. No sooner had he started to play with it than it bounced off the wall and hit his mother's vase, knocking it over and down onto the floor.

Flurry cringed as he saw what was taking place. The entire event seemed to unfold in slow motion, right before his very eyes. The shattering sound was so loud that Flurry jumped and dove under the couch to hide. He peeked out to see the mess he had made. Seeing the broken shards of pottery and dirt strewn across the floor, Flurry knew that he might not be going outside for a very long time. "Uh oh!" exclaimed Flurry.

Fast-paced footsteps could be heard coming into the room. "Flurry! What was that?" Flurry's mother came rushing into the room. "Oh, Flurry! What did you do?"

Climbing out from under the couch Flurry began to cry. Running up to hug his mother, he cried, "I'm sorry, Mama, I didn't mean to. I was bored. I wanted to play with my ball, and it accidentally hit the vase. I didn't mean to. I'm sorry."

Mrs. Snow saw Flurry's cute little face, all drenched with tears, and her heart melted. "Oh, my little dear, come here." Flurry squeezed tighter as she continued to embrace him and comfort him.

Mrs. Snow took a seat on the couch as she listened to Flurry continue, "I don't mean to get into trouble, Mama, honest. I feel like I'm always disappointing you and papa. I'm so sorry." He kept sobbing and now had a tear soaked scarf in addition to his tear soaked fur.

Holding Flurry on her lap, she attempted to comfort him. "It's okay, my sweetheart, accidents happen. I have an idea! Why don't you go to the grocery store and pick up some items for your mother while I clean up the mess and start preparing dinner. That way you can get out of the house for a bit. Does that sound okay to you?"

"Uh huh!" sobbed Flurry as he wiped his tears away.

"Good! Now go get ready, and I'll make a list."

Flurry hopped down off his mother's lap and quickly ran off and returned very shortly after his mother finished writing out her grocery list. However, Flurry ran right past her and bolted out the door. He was so happy that he was getting out of the house that he forgot what he was going out for.

Before he got too far out the door, his mother cleared her throat to get his attention. "Aren't you forgetting something?" asked his mother.

"Oh yeah!" he exclaimed, as he ran back and hugged her saying, "I love you, Mama.

Okay, goodbye!" He then returned to his mission of heading straight for the door again.

Amused, Mrs. Snow chuckled and said, "Yes, that was very sweet of you, but that wasn't what I meant. Aren't you forgetting something else? I'll give you a hint. It starts with an L, ends in a T, and has an I and an S in the middle."

Flurry looked back to see his mother waving a piece of paper in her paw. "Oh yeah! Sorry!" Flurry ran back up to his mother and got the list from her. He then called out, "Okay, goodbye!" and rushed out the door. Just as before, Flurry was off in a hurry, only turning back for a moment to wave to his mother.

Flurry's mother waved goodbye. She had a smile on her face, amused by how adorable her son could be. Then suddenly she thought to herself, "I hope he doesn't get into any more trouble."

On the way to the shop, Flurry kept imagining what it would be like to purchase groceries like the grownups do. He was picturing how happy his mother would be and how proud his father would be. Flurry didn't even notice all the other children playing. He was on a mission of the utmost importance and nothing could distract him.

Flurry arrived at the store. Being so small, he had to wait outside for an older bear to come out, so he could slip in. Being inside, Flurry felt a sense of awe, as the store was filled with so many goodies, many of which were beyond his reach. Flurry had been to the grocery store many times with his parents, but this was his first time on his own. He felt so proud, like he was a grownup.

On his way into the store a stack of honey jars caught his attention. "Oooh!" Flurry exclaimed. He was mesmerized by the sheer number of them as they towered over him. Flurry looked at his list, "Mama didn't put honey on the list, but I'm sure she'll appreciate my thoughtfulness if I bring one home for her. It'll be a gift to show her how much I love her."

Without hesitation, Flurry reached for one of the honey jars at the bottom of the stack and removed it. Flurry wasn't sure what happened next, as it happened so quickly. One moment Flurry was grocery shopping, and the next moment there were broken jars of honey spilled all over him and the store floor. The storekeeper was so angry and all the other shoppers stared at Flurry. Feeling humiliated, Flurry began to cry and ran out of the store as quickly as he could.

Flurry ran home as fast as his little legs would take him. He entered his home and ran up to his mother, crying his eyes out. "Mama! Mama! I was … I … I wanted … I wanted to do something good for you *sniffle* and then the honey fell *sniffle* and then everyone got angry *sniffle* and then …" Between Flurry's crying and sniffles, it was like trying to decipher a code. Mrs. Snow could tell something went horribly wrong and that it involved honey, as Flurry was covered in it.

"Flurry, calm down! I tell you what, go get the bathtub ready and I'll be in to give you a bath in just a moment."

"Okay," Flurry answered as he walked away, sniffling and rubbing his eyes.

Mrs. Snow entered the bathroom to help Flurry take his bath. She was finishing up with Flurry's bath when she heard voices outside on the sidewalk. She peeked out from the window to see the storekeeper and Mr. Snow having a conversation. She could faintly make out the storekeeper's words, "You're a good bear Mr. Snow, but your cub needs some discipline."

Mr. Snow came in the front door and then turned back to say goodnight to the storekeeper. Flurry heard the door close and immediately submersed himself in the tub water.

"Now, sweetie, don't be like that," his mother pleaded with him, as she lifted him back up by his arm. Flurry cringed, as he could hear his father's footsteps grow louder, as each step drew nearer and nearer, up the wooden steps of the stairway. Quickly, Flurry gathered the soap bubbles from his bath and heaped them up over his head to hide himself.

There was a light knock at the bathroom door. "Where is he?" Mr. Snow asked.

Mrs. Snow rushed to the door, slipped out into the hallway, and closed the bathroom door behind her. "Now, honey, Flurry's had a rough day. I'll handle it. All I want to know is, how bad it is?"

"Well, the storekeeper owed me some favors for fixing up his shop last winter, so we called it even. I offered to have Flurry sent over to clean up the mess for him, but he insists that I not let Flurry get anywhere near his shop. I think he's afraid that Flurry will find himself in more trouble."

Mrs. Snow's face dropped a bit, "Poor

little guy. He has a big heart and he means well. I wonder what we can do to keep him out of trouble?"

"Hmmmm …" Mr. Snow put his paw on his chin, as he thought about the matter. "Maybe we should bring the matter to Chris," Mr. Snow suggested. "Yes, I think I'll take him to Chris's house tomorrow and see what he suggests."

With the matter settled, Mr. Snow called it a night. Mrs. Snow attended to finishing up with Flurry's bath and then had a late dinner after tucking Flurry into bed. She read Flurry a bedtime story, and it was off to bed for everyone in the Snow family's household. Mrs. Snow gave her boy a hug and a kiss on the cheek. She stroked the tuft fur on his forehead and said to him, "Don't be sad, my little darling, everything will work out. Now get some rest, you have a big day ahead of you tomorrow. Who knows? Maybe there'll be a surprise too."

"Ooh! I love surprises! What is it, Mama?" Flurry asked with such passion.

"Now, now, it's time for bed. Sleep well, and I'll see my sweetie when he wakes up. I love you," his mother said as she turned out the light.

"I love you, too! Okay, goodbye!" Flurry answered her as he pulled the warm blanket up to his chin. Flurry felt comforted and began to wonder what tomorrow would bring, but it wasn't long before he drifted off to sleep and had wonderful dreams of tasty treats and epic adventures.

# Chapter 3
## MR. KRINGLE

The following morning arrived, but Flurry, sitting up in bed and rubbing his eyes, thought the sun had arrived far too quickly. After all, he needed his beauty rest. However, his attitude quickly changed when he heard something he didn't expect.

"Flurry! Hurry up and get ready. We're going to go visit Mr. Kringle today." Flurry's father called up to him from the foot of the stairway.

Flurry sat straight up in bed as if an electric current had shot through his body. He quickly threw the blanket off and jumped out of bed. Flurry's excitement couldn't be contained. He was in such a hurry that he nearly fell down multiple times before reaching his father. It was as if Flurry's little legs couldn't get him there fast enough.

Flurry darted down the steps, blew past his father, and was already at the door before being halted in his tracks. "Whoa! Hold on there, little fella!" exclaimed Flurry's father. "Where's the fire?"

"Indeed! You haven't even had breakfast, not to mention that you didn't give me a hug," Flurry's mother interjected.

"Aw, but Mama, I want to see Santa!" Flurry whined.

"Now, you know he doesn't like to be

called 'Santa,' don't you? His proper name is Christopher or Mr. Kringle to you," Flurry's father corrected.

"Oh yeah! I forgot. Sorry." Flurry came up to his mother and gave her leg a hug, while she finished cooking breakfast for the family.

"Okay, breakfast is ready." Flurry's mother prepared their plates, and they had breakfast together at the table.

Now Flurry loved food very much and would normally not pass up a meal, but his excitement to see Mr. Kringle surpassed his love for food. Mr. Kringle was very good with kids, and Flurry always loved to see him. Flurry didn't yet know why they would make the trip to Mr. Kringle's house so early in the morning, but none of that mattered. All that mattered was that Flurry would get to see "Santa."

After finishing up his meal, Flurry gave his mother a big hug and a kiss. Mrs. Snow felt so loved as she got another round of hugs and kisses from her beloved husband also. As her boys began their exit, she said, "Have a good day, my boys, and, Flurry, behave."

"I will, Mama!" Flurry said in a confident and assuring voice while nodding his head.

Mr. Snow waved goodbye as he closed the door behind them. Mrs. Snow watched from the window with a smile, observing Flurry pulling on his father's arm in an attempt to make him walk faster. Flurry was a very excitable, young cub, and his presence always livened the mood anywhere he went.

The path to the Kringle household was very beautiful that morning. The fresh snow sparkled like glitter, and the sun cast long shadows of the evergreen trees across the curves of the landscape. The birds were chirping, and the absence of wind made the morning feel serene. The stillness of their surroundings made the sound of their footsteps sound like they were stomping as they marched down the snow-covered cobblestone path.

They had only been on the path for a short while before Flurry stopped dead in his tracks. "What's the matter, son?" his father asked.

Flurry spun around and began to run back toward the house. Being quick on his feet, Mr. Snow reached out and snagged Flurry's scarf. He found himself amused as he watched Flurry running in place. "Slow down there, my boy. What has you troubled?" he asked.

"I forgot to draw a picture for him. I don't

want to go without drawing him a picture." Flurry answered, as he kept attempting to escape his father's strong grip on his scarf.

"Mr. Kringle will understand. It'll be okay. How about this? Next time you can make two drawings for him. Okay?" Mr. Snow reasoned with Flurry and won.

"Okay." Flurry answered as he stopped struggling, quickly spun around, and took off toward the Kringle household again.

"What has gotten into you?" Mr. Snow asked.

"Well, now we have to make up for lost time. Hurry, Papa!" Flurry explained.

Mr. Snow smiled as he admired his son while also trying to catch up with him. "Slow down!" he shouted to his son, who was quickly about to vanish around the tree up ahead of them.

For Flurry, the walk to Mr. Kringle's home got more exciting with each step. Flurry kept imagining what they would say to each other and whether or not Mr. Kringle would have any goodies. Flurry loved all manner of sweets, especially anything made of chocolate. Flurry's mouth watered as he thought of hot chocolate and fresh, moist chocolate chip cookies.

Before Flurry realized it, they had arrived at Mr. Kringle's house. Mr. Kringle's house was quite a sight to see. It was very large with many rooms. To Flurry, the house was like a castle. Flurry had often dreamed of exploring such a magnificent structure some day. The possibilities of adventure in such a place seemed endless. "Oh, if only Sunny and Bliz could see this," Flurry thought to himself. Bliz was another of Flurry's close friends as well as his cousin.

Walking up to the front door, Flurry's size really came into perspective for him. Granted, Flurry was just a teddy bear cub, small enough for a child to carry, but Mr. Kringle was a very tall man. Mr. Kringle was more than six feet tall, so when Flurry stood before the front door, it seemed as if a giant might live in the house.

"Are you going to knock?" asked Flurry's father.

Flurry was now nervous. He wasn't sure why, but he was. He inched forward and raised his right paw. He closed his eyes and made a knocking motion, but he didn't feel his paw connect with the door, nor did he hear a knocking sound. He opened his eyes and looked up to see Mr. Kringle standing right in front of him. Mr. Kringle had already opened the door before Flurry had the chance to knock.

"Well hello there, little fellow. I've been expecting you." Mr. Kringle spoke to Flurry in a warm and inviting voice.

The nervousness went away and Flurry was now excited to see Mr. Kringle. Flurry ran forward and hugged his leg. Mr. Kringle bent down and lifted Flurry up onto his shoulders. "Weeeee!" Flurry cried out as he giggled with excitement.

"Mr. Snow, welcome! Welcome! Please come in." Mr. Kringle outstretched his arm in the direction of his home's interior.

Mr. Snow shook off the loose snow from his feet and entered. Stepping inside, Mr. Snow's eyes opened wide to take in the view. The house had a fireplace, comfortable-looking furniture, and many tapestries.

Closing the door behind him, Mr. Kringle spoke, "Can I interest you in something to drink, perhaps some hot chocolate?"

Before Mr. Snow could answer, Flurry had already chimed in, "I want some!"

"No, thank you. I'm fine," answered Mr. Snow, as he sat in the seat nearest to the fireplace.

"Sweetheart, would you be so kind as to bring out some hot chocolate and some fresh cookies for our much welcomed guests?" Mr. Kringle asked his middle-aged wife. She had long, red hair, a slender face, and green eyes. By most standards, she would be regarded as very beautiful.

"Why, certainly. Do you want marshmallows in your hot chocolate, Flurry?" asked Mrs. Kringle.

"Sure! Yum, yum!" Flurry enthusiastically

replied.

Mr. Kringle chuckled. Flurry was a source of great amusement and adoration. Mr. Kringle sat down in his seat at a three-quarters angle to Flurry. This position was directly across from Mr. Snow, who sat in the other seat at the opposite end of the coffee table positioned between them. Flurry sat on the couch. He had the whole thing to himself. He could look right at the fireplace from across the coffee table.

Flurry was enamored with Mr. Kringle's appearance. Mr. Kringle wore a long, crimson-colored coat that extended to the middle of his thighs. The coat was adorned with gold trim along the hem and was very decorative along the opening. This coat was the most eye-catching part of his attire. Besides the coat he wore a sky blue shirt, a forest green scarf, black pants, and dark brown boots.

It was at this time that Mrs. Kringle brought out the treats. Flurry was so excited that he started guzzling the hot chocolate. Mr. Kringle chuckled again, "Slow down there, boy. There's plenty. No need to rush."

Flurry pulled the steaming mug away from his face to reveal a hot chocolate mustache that had formed on his upper lip. Both of the Kringles and Mr. Snow laughed. "I can see that he's just as adorable as ever," observed Mrs. Kringle.

"Well, we have his mother to thank for that," Mr. Snow answered.

Mr. Kringle cleared his throat and in a more solemn tone said, "Well then, let's get down to business, shall we? I hear you've been having some trouble with this little one."

Flurry had been in the process of eating a cookie when he suddenly froze, mouth wide open, and he dropped the cookie from his paw. Flurry had been tricked, or so he thought. "Wait a minute! What do you mean? What does he mean, Papa?" Flurry looked back and forth between the other two males, sitting at each side of the table opposite from him.

Mr. Kringle interjected, "Don't worry dear Flurry, we're here to help you, not to punish you."

Flurry couldn't believe his ears. He was in shock. He thought they were going to have a day of fun, not a day of being lectured. Flurry lost his appetite and put the cookie that he had dropped in his lap back on the plate.

Mr. Snow began, "Thank you for meeting

with us under such short notice. I didn't know what else to do, so my wife and I thought that you might have a solution to our dilemma."

"Well, I can't make any promises, but I'll do my best to give you sound advice," Mr. Kringle answered, as he grabbed his chin, leaned forward, and gave his full attention to Mr. Snow.

Mr. Snow continued, "You see, Flurry has a big heart, and he means well, but he just keeps getting himself into trouble." Mr. Snow went on for a while, reciting examples, such as the recent events of tree climbing, breaking the vase, and toppling the pile of honey jars at the grocery store.

After Mr. Snow had exhausted all of his examples, Mr. Kringle turned to Flurry with his deep brown eyes. Flurry looked up and their gazes met. Flurry could see the empathy in Mr. Kringle's eyes.

Mr. Kringle stroked his dark, graying beard and spoke up, "Flurry, come here, little fellow. Sit on my lap." Mr. Kringle patted his lap twice to indicate where he wanted Flurry to sit.

Flurry climbed down from the couch and scurried up to Mr. Kringle. Flurry held up his arms, as if trying to reach something on a high shelf. Mr. Kringle reached down, picked Flurry up, and set him on his lap. "Let's hear your version of this story, shall we?"

Flurry's mouth seemed to move a mile a minute as he detailed every event that took place and how he had gotten into so many messes. By the time Flurry got through all of his stories, he was in tears.

"I didn't mean to get into trouble. I just

wanted to play and have fun." Flurry struggled to get the words out between sobs.

Tears formed in Christopher's eyes, and he reached over and wiped Flurry's tears away. "Flurry, I tell you what. How about I give you a job?"

"A job? Wow! What kind of job?" Flurry was so excited at the idea. It was as if he hadn't even been crying. It's funny how a cubs' emotions can change so quickly and they act as if the previous emotional state hadn't even happened.

Mr. Snow was surprised by what Mr. Kringle had to say. After all of the time they spent talking with him, giving Flurry a job didn't seem like the logical conclusion to the troublesome situation Mr. Snow was in.

Mr. Kringle spoke up, "Well, as I see it, I think that giving you some responsibilities might be of some help. I think putting your gifts and talents to good use can benefit you greatly. Having responsibilities will occupy your time and help you to set priorities. You're talented, creative, and you have a big heart. You like to give joy to others, so why not put you in charge of my teddy bear production line at the toy factory? There you can influence the teddy bear toy line and have a say in what the teddy bears look like before we produce and ship them to the toy stores. What do you say to that?"

Flurry's jaw practically hit the floor. "Wow! That would be really great!"

"Okay, then! You start first thing tomorrow morning. I expect you to be at the factory, bright and early. One of the workers, named Jinja, will greet you at the door and give you a tour of the facility. If you have any questions, Jinja can answer them for you," instructed Mr. Kringle.

Mr. Kringle stood up and carried Flurry to the front door before setting him down. Mr. Snow followed behind them before saying, "Thank you so much for listening to us. I hope your idea will work. Thank you for such a great opportunity."

Mr. Kringle began, "You're more than welcome, Mr. Snow. If you ever need anything, don't hesitate to ask …"

Before Christopher could finish his thought, Flurry quickly cut in, "Oh! In that case, may I have another cookie?"

"Flurry! I taught you better than that!" Mr. Snow spoke in a reprimanding voice. "Besides, I don't think that's what he meant."

Christopher erupted in laughter. Mr. Snow and Flurry didn't expect that reaction. "Of course you can! Take the rest of them. I'm not expecting any more visitors for a while, and I'm trying to watch my waist line, if you know what I mean. If you don't take them, I might eat them all myself." Mr. Kringle continued chuckling as Mrs. Kringle brought out a little bag that she had filled with the remaining cookies.

"What do you say?" Mr. Snow asked his son.

"Thank you Santa!" Flurry answered.

Christopher paused, while he thought about what to say. "You know, my name is Christopher. If you keep saying 'Santa,' that's going to catch on and everyone will be calling me that."

"Oh, sorry. I forgot," Flurry apologized.

"It's all right. I'm pleased to see your countenance improve. Enjoy your day and

Jinja will see you at the factory tomorrow morning.

"Okay, goodbye!" said Flurry, with much vigor in his voice. They both waved farewell to each other, and Flurry kept looking over his shoulder until Christopher finally closed the door behind him. Flurry was gleeful, and his joy was so radiant that you would almost swear that he was glowing like the sun.

Flurry munched on his cookies, getting chocolate all around his mouth and crumbs on his scarf, while thinking about what it would be like at the toy factory. At that moment, nothing else in the world mattered. Flurry was at peace as he walked home with his father, happy and content, eating his chocolate chip cookies.

# Chapter 4
## THE TOY FACTORY

The next day couldn't come soon enough. Flurry barely got an ounce of sleep. He spent the night imagining what the next day would be like. He imagined things like what he would make the teddy bears look like, what he would call them, and how he would spend all day playing with them.

Early the next morning while it was still dark, Flurry sat up, wide eyed and bushy tailed – or at least he would have if he had a tail. He was raring to go and was on his feet before his parents had even opened their eyes. However, Flurry had a way of making sure you were up when he needed you to be.

Flurry ran to his parents' bedroom door and pushed it open. As the door creaked open, letting a beam of orange light into the room, a long, dark, and furry shadow was cast along the floorboards and up onto the bed of two sleeping teddy bears.

Mr. and Mrs. Snow remained asleep. Flurry thought this to be strange since they both knew it was his big day. "Why wouldn't they be up to send me on my way?" he wondered.

Well, that didn't stop Flurry from making sure they were awake. The sound of panting could be heard as Flurry climbed up the bed. He rushed over and gave a gentle push on his mother's shoulder, "Mama! Mama! Time to get up!" Unfortunately, there wasn't a response. Flurry turned to his father and tugged on his ear, "Papa! Papa! I have to go to work!" More snoring was the only response Flurry got.

Not to go unnoticed, Flurry began jumping up and down calling out, "Wake up! Wake up! Wake up!"

"Ah!" screamed Mr. and Mrs. Snow as they shot up, startled, having come close to falling out of the bed.

Flurry's parents were both flustered, and understandably so. Nobody likes to be rallied from sleep in that manner. "Flurry! Do you know what time it is? Why are you waking us up so early?" Flurry's father shouted.

"I have to go to work now. Just thought I'd let you know. Okay, goodbye!" Flurry quickly spoke and then hopped down off their bed.

"Sweetie, you don't have to go to work for another three hours. Go back to bed," Mrs. Snow told Flurry as she yawned.

Flurry seemed surprised. His excitement and impatience blinded him from the fact that the sun hadn't risen yet. "Aw!" moped Flurry as he slowly shuffled back out of the room, leaving the door open behind him.

With a sigh, Mrs. Snow got out of bed. She looked back at her husband, who was also getting out of bed. "No. Just stay there. You need your rest. I'll go check on Flurry." Mrs. Snow gently pushed her husband back down in the bed and pulled the blanket back up over him. She kissed him on the cheek, and he was fast asleep again by the time she reached the door.

Mrs. Snow came down the hallway and peeked into Flurry's room. He was impatiently pacing back and forth beside his bed. "Sweetie, I understand that you're excited, but you can't rush the rising of the sun."

"I wish I could. I wish it were time to go already!" Flurry exclaimed.

Suddenly, without any explanation, it got brighter outside and the sun was now peeking up from the eastern horizon. "That's strange!" exclaimed Mrs. Snow. "Flurry, do you see that?"

Flurry ran up to the window and peeked out. "Wow! It's time to go! That's amazing!" Flurry's countenance improved and his excitement rekindled.

Mrs. Snow was very perplexed by the sudden sunrise. In all her life, she had never seen something so strange. The North Pole truly was a mysterious place but nothing like that had ever happened before.

Flurry ran back to his father's bedroom to wake him up again. "Papa! Papa! It's time to get up!"

"Flurry, you were just in here only a few minutes ago," Flurry's father answered in a frustrated voice. You could hear a bit of a growl as he spoke.

Mrs. Snow walked in behind Flurry and grabbed her boy by the shoulders to back him away from the bed. "Calm down, Flurry," she said.

"Okay, Mama, sorry." Flurry answered. Flurry continued to stand quietly with his arms behind his back. He looked ever so adorable.

"Flurry's right, it's time to get up. I have

no explanation for it. The sun just suddenly did in minutes what should have taken it hours to do," Mrs. Snow told her husband.

"That's odd," said Mr. Snow, as he sat up and rubbed his eyes. He then got out of the bed, walked over to the window, and looked out. Sure enough, the sun was just coming up over the horizon. "That's the strangest thing I've ever seen. I'll have to ask Christopher what he makes of this." Flurry's parents exchanged concerned glances at each other before Mr. Snow shrugged his shoulders and put on his bowtie.

"Papa, come on! I'm going to be late!" Flurry's voice was riddled with deep concern. Flurry didn't want to mess up his first day on the job. He wanted to make Mr. Kringle and his parents proud of him.

All three of the bears went downstairs and

Mrs. Snow fixed Flurry some breakfast and sack lunches for both her son and her husband. Before leaving, Flurry gave his mother a hug, then off to the front door he went.

Before Flurry and his father were but a few steps from the house, Mrs. Snow came and stood at the threshold of the door and waved to them as they walked down the cobblestone path.

"Have a good day, my sweethearts!" she called out to them.

"Thank you! We will!" they both hollered back to her in unison. Flurry walked backwards so he could wave back to his mother as she continued to wave to him.

"Okay, goodbye!" Flurry called back to his mother, who looked so proud of him. It warmed Flurry's heart and made him even more dedicated to doing his best at the toy factory.

Mr. Snow and his son traveled the winding path up and down gradual slopes of the landscape. The walk to the factory was a long one but certainly very scenic. The workings of a beautiful day were at hand, but this morning things weren't as they should be. The village seemed to be in chaos as the teddy bears ran all around trying to get ready for the day. It was as if everyone had overslept and were now frantic to make it to their destinations on time. Mr. Snow had never seen anything like this before.

Uncertain of what else to do, they continued down the hill into the valley, where the toy factory was positioned next to a winding river. The factory was small and the only landmark to be found in the valley on that side of the river. A thick forest sat at the opposite riverbank. On a normal day, Flurry would have seen the forest as a place to be explored and the promise of adventure would've beckoned to him but not today. Today, Flurry's mind was set on the impact he could make on the teddy bear production line.

As they approached the factory, they could see many teddy bears rushing to get inside. Christopher Kringle stood outside the front doors, greeting the teddy bears as they came in. Seeing Christopher was a welcome sight. Christopher had a smile on his face, spoke calmly, and frequently chuckled. "No worries, my friends, everything is fine. We're just off to a late start today, nothing to get too flustered about."

As Mr. Snow and Flurry drew near, Mr.

Kringle also addressed them, "Well, hello there! I'm proud to see the two of you here this fine morning." After greeting them, he turned his attention to Flurry. Squatting down to be closer to Flurry's eye level, Christopher said, "It does my heart joy to see you here, my little friend. Are you excited to be here?"

"Uh huh!" Flurry exclaimed and shook his head up and down vigorously.

Christopher chuckled and continued, "Well, I should be headed back toward home. Jinja will be here shortly. As you can see, this day has started off rather unconventionally." Christopher then tipped his cap to Mr. Snow, "Good day to you, Mr. Snow."

"Good day to you too, Mr. Kringle," he answered.

"Flurry, be sure to have fun and be good,"

Christopher directed, as he glanced back toward Flurry, while continuing his walk up the icy path.

"I will! Okay, goodbye!" Flurry fervently waved to Mr. Kringle and then focused his attention back on his father.

"Flurry, I have to go in and work now. Just wait here and Jinja will surely be out to greet you soon," Flurry's father spoke as he gave Flurry a warm hug. "I'm proud of you, son. Have a good day at work. I love you."

"Thank you, Papa. I love you too!" Flurry called back to his father as he vanished behind the closing factory doors.

Flurry didn't have to wait very long before the door opened again and a bear with red fur, glasses, and a mug of coffee came to greet him. "Hello. I'm Jinja. You must be Flurry."

"Yes, I am," Flurry said as he stared at the yellow crescent moon shape on Jinja's chest. Jinja looked a bit unique from other teddy bears Flurry had seen. The individual responsible for creating Jinja wanted him to resemble a moon bear. Moon bears have a crescent moon shape on their chests; that's why they are called "moon" bears.

Jinja was one of Mr. Kringle's most trusted workers. Jinja was hard working, dedicated, and easy going. He primarily did most of his work with clay and pottery and had a reputation for always having his mug of coffee close at hand.

"Please, come in. You must be cold standing out here." Jinja spoke in a concerned voice.

"I'm fine. I was just playing in the snow," Flurry assured him.

Flurry entered through the main entrance, and Jinja closed the doors behind them. It was nice and warm inside, and Flurry felt even more ardent than before – if that's possible. He could hear other teddy bears humming, whistling or singing while they built a variety of different toys and dolls. Many of the toys were to be given as gifts at Christmas to all of the children in the world. Yet, some of the toys were also sent to toy stores around the world. The money from the toys helped Christopher purchase materials that he and the teddy bears would need on a day-to-day basis.

Before Flurry had much of a chance to take it all in, another bear came to greet him. This bear was very big and round. He looked a lot like a panda bear, but instead of black and white, this bear was purple and white. He had on a tool belt, similar to what Flurry's father wore, but this belt held mechanic tools instead of carpentry tools.

"Flurry, I'd like you to meet my close friend Mojo. Mojo is responsible for repairing everything here at the …" Jinja didn't get to finish what he was saying before Mojo interrupted him.

"Not everything!" Mojo interjected.

"Well, everything mechanical," Jinja quickly corrected himself.

"Well, technically, I just repair the equipment," Mojo commented.

"Why do you always have to correct me?" Jinja shot back.

"I don't always correct you," Mojo replied.

"Yes, you do!" said Jinja.

"I only correct you when you are wrong,"

Mojo replied, this time putting his paws on his hips.

"You correct me all the time," Jinja insisted and now looked flustered.

"Then I guess you are always wrong," Mojo returned in a smug voice and with a smirk on his face.

"Oh no you didn't! How could you say that?" answered Jinja, now in a voice of shock and disbelief. If Jinja's fur weren't already red, it would be easier to see how flushed his face had become.

"I just did," answered Mojo.

"It's always the same with you. You always start arguments with me," Jinja continued.

"I'm not arguing," Mojo assured.

"Yes, you are!"

"No, I'm not!"

In the midst of their debate, Flurry began to feel that it wasn't anywhere near to being over, so he slipped by them and away from the argument. Flurry then decided it best to just give himself the grand tour.

Flurry went from room to room and observed all the grand craftsmanship that went into each and every toy. The other teddy bears were such fine craftsmen, and Flurry marveled at all the wonderful toys that he secretly desired to play with.

Flurry had already toured the entire plant and was at the boxing and shipping end of the factory when Jinja finally caught up with him.

"There you are!" Jinja exclaimed. "I've been looking all over for you. Where have you been?" Jinja came jogging up to Flurry. He stood by Flurry panting and pushed his glasses back up, as they had slid down his nose a bit.

"Well, I didn't want to interrupt your argument, so I gave myself the tour," a now reserved Flurry answered.

"Oh! That. Well, he always does that. It's not a big deal." Jinja shrugged off the incident as if it weren't worth mentioning. He took a sip of his coffee and then pointed to the shipping line and said, "Well, as you can see, this is where we box and ship all of our toys out. Someday you'll get to see your very own toy designs being shipped from here."

Flurry was already imagining it, while observing the boxes being drug along in front of him on the conveyor belt.

Jinja continued, "But remember. Safety first. You don't want to get too close to the conveyor belt. If you were to fall onto the belt, you might get boxed up and shipped off. That would be very bad!"

Flurry immediately stepped away from the railing, and he suddenly felt fearful to go anywhere near the conveyor belt. As Jinja walked on, to continue the last leg of the tour, Flurry quickly chased after him, not wanting to be left alone anywhere near the conveyor belt.

Flurry's first day on the job was a blast. He enjoyed meeting the other teddy bears and being shown around the factory.

Flurry quickly filled in his role as the lead input advisor on Christopher Kringle's teddy bear assembly line. Flurry would give his ideas and input into the creation of the teddy bears in a way that only a cub could. Christopher Kringle was wise to have Flurry there, giving his input. If you want to make something a child will like, you ask a child.

It's uncertain how long Flurry was a worker at the factory. It could've been weeks, months, or even years. It's as the saying goes, "Time flies when you're having fun." And Flurry was certainly having fun. He especially liked quality control. That was a fancy way of saying, "Play with the toys."

Flurry did his job well, and things were about to become even better after his epiphany.

One night, while lying in bed, Flurry had an excellent idea. His idea was so amazing that Flurry wondered why he hadn't thought of it before. Flurry thought to himself, "If I'm the cutest teddy bear ever, and everyone loves me, then why not make teddy bears that look like me? They'll be the most popular item ever!" Now, we all have character flaws and Flurry had his own, just like anyone else might. Flurry's biggest character flaw was that he could be overly vain about his physical appearance. So many had praised him for his cute looks that it had gone to his head. Flurry was in need of some humility and would get some in the most unexpected way.

Flurry had been quick to implement his new teddy bear line. He named them the Flakey line. The Flakey bears looked exactly like Flurry, and Flurry was supremely confident that they would become Mr. Kringle's hottest selling item.

One night, as Flurry was locking up, he was thinking about the Flakey teddy bear line. He was so proud of what he had achieved that he decided to go back inside and take another look at them before going home.

Flurry walked back into the toy factory, the doors shutting behind him. He skipped through the factory, occasionally stopping to look at a toy. He then went into the shipping area where the Flakey bears were being boxed up and shipped to toy stores.

Flurry felt so proud of himself. He had done a good job, stayed out of trouble, made his parents proud, lived up to Mr. Kringle's expectations, and made the cutest teddy bears ever – other than himself, of course.

Flurry was imagining being famous and everyone carrying their very own Flakey bears around with them. His head was up in the clouds so high that he forgot Jinja's warning about not getting too close to the conveyor belt. Normally, Flurry would never go near it, but he had forgotten about it in his moment of self-adoration.

Flurry could hear the automated boxing taking place. Giant mechanical arms repeated the motion of picking up and placing Flakey bears into the large boxes and sealing them up, while the bears came gliding down a slide and onto the conveyor belt.

It was difficult for Flurry to see over the guard rail – he's pretty small, after all. Flurry climbed up each rung of the barrier between himself and the conveyor belt below and peered over to watch the process taking place.

Flurry admired his creation and thought about how cute he was. Before Flurry even realized what was going on, he lost his balance and fell onto the conveyor belt. Flurry panicked and was attempting to get down from the conveyor belt when a large metal hand came down, snatched Flurry up, and placed him in a box with the other Flakey bears.

Flurry screamed and shouted for help, but nobody could hear him. Everyone had left for the night, and the toy factory had a policy that nobody was ever to be alone near the running equipment. Flurry broke that rule and was now in a lot of trouble.

Flurry toiled to climb up out of the box, but every time he made some progress, another Flakey bear was dropped into the box right on top of him, knocking him down from the progress he had just made.

Flurry continued to call out for help, but no ear could hear him and he was all alone in the box full of Flakey bears. Flurry continued to struggle and climb. He began to have a glimmer of hope when he was near the top of the box and no more Flakey bears were being added to the collection, but his hope was quickly doused when the box started to move and the flaps came up and then closed down over Flurry. It was suddenly dark and the only thing Flurry could see was a thin line of light, where the flaps met. Then that tiny bit of light was quickly extinguished as the sound of packaging tape could be heard, and Flurry was sealed in the box labeled to be shipped to a far off country named Middleasia.

# Chapter 5
## TOY STORE CHASE

Darkness and despair overtook Flurry as he lay among the Flakey bears without hope of getting out. Flurry regretted his actions and wished he hadn't gone back into the factory to marvel at himself. There's no telling how long Flurry had been laying among the other Flakey bears, for he had no way of distinguishing the passing of time in the pitch black clutches of darkness in the sealed box.

He felt hungry, but that was purely in his

mind because teddy bears have no need for food; eating is simply recreational. However, Flurry loved the taste of delicious food, and now he missed it more than ever. Flurry began to visualize the delectable tastes of freshly baked sugar cookies, the peppermint flavor of candy canes, and the creamy goodness of hot chocolate. It was almost unbearable.

Flurry continued to lay among the soft fur of the lifeless Flakey bears. He thought about his parents and how much he missed them. As he thought about his mother and father, he began to cry. Tears streamed down his face as remorse and regret overwhelmed him. Flurry wanted to go back home again, but he was trapped.

At the North Pole, things weren't much better. Mr. and Mrs. Snow quickly noticed the absence of their deeply loved son. It wasn't like Flurry to not be home on time. Their worry quickly turned into action. They went to the factory in search of him, but found it closed up and the lights out. Mr. Kringle joined the search while he and a search team of teddy bears combed the factory, but they were too late. The boxes had been shipped out already and not a single one of them would have ever guessed to look for Flurry there.

They searched the factory from top to bottom, but turned up nothing, not even a clue as to what had happened to Flurry. They were about to abandon the search when Jinja noticed something odd. The automated process for packaging the Flakey bears hadn't ever been known to make a mistake in the packaging of teddy bears. The machines kept an accurate count of how many bears were packed into each box. Each box would be filled with one hundred teddy bears before being shipped out. However, one Flakey bear had been left behind. Jinja and Mojo stood over the lone Flakey bear that remained. They looked at it laying on the conveyor belt and contemplated the meaning of its presence. This was perplexing, to say the least, for there shouldn't have been any Flakey bears left over.

Jinja quickly brought this newfound clue to the attention of Mr. Kringle, and the rest of the teddy bear search team. "Oh my!" Flurry's mother gasped. "You don't suppose Flurry was in one of the boxes being shipped off, do you?" she tried to ask, while struggling to hold back her tears. She wasn't able to hold them back for very long. Mrs.

Snow began to tear up, and her husband put his arm around her as he too fought back tears of his own.

Mr. Kringle felt deep empathy for them and tried to comfort Mrs. Snow by saying, "There's no need to worry, my dear. If Flurry has been shipped out with the teddy bears, he will turn up at one of the toy stores. From there, we can retrieve him. He'll be fine." His words were well meaning, but they weren't encouraging enough to stop the tears that were now freely flowing from her eyes.

"Well, there's nothing we can do until the packages reach their destinations. Then we will know where Flurry has arrived and we can act accordingly. For now, we can keep Flurry in our thoughts." Mr. Kringle concluded their meeting and escorted the bears out the front doors before locking up.

It's uncertain how long Flurry and his parents cried as they thought about and missed each other. For Flurry, though, his crying was abruptly halted when he felt a sharp jolt. The box suddenly stopped moving, and he could hear the faint sound of voices. He couldn't recognize the muffled voices through the box and the other teddy bears piled on top of him.

Flurry began to feel relieved and thought to himself, "It must be one of the other workers. They found me! I'm saved!"

Flurry's excitement continued to grow as different sounds permeated the box where he lay in wait. He could hear the sounds of cutting and the removal of packaging tape. A sliver of light shone into the box. Then, in an instance, light flooded into the box, as the flaps were opened wide. Flurry jumped up impassioned and exclaimed, "Here I am! Yay! I'm saved!"

To Flurry's surprise, he wasn't in the toy factory or even at the North Pole. The box openers weren't teddy bears or Mr. Kringle either. Flurry looked in disbelief at some men in matching red shirts that read, "Middleasia's Toy Emporium."

Flurry then realized that the outside world isn't accustomed to seeing a living, breathing, speaking teddy bear. Flurry instantly fell back into the box and lay as still as he possibly could. As he lay among the Flakey bears, as stiff as a board, Flurry wondered, "Did they notice me? I hope they didn't notice." However, it's difficult to not notice a teddy bear jump up out of a box and speak to you.

The shock and awe of seeing a living

teddy bear was almost palpable. You could have heard a pin drop in the still silence of the room. The toy store workers were contemplating if the teddy bear had a voice box installed or if it really was alive. After all, if it really was a living teddy bear, this could be their lucky break. They could sell Flurry for a very high price if word got out that he was actually a living, breathing teddy bear. This was unprecedented.

Realizing the money they could make from this discovery, the workers all rushed to the box. Luckily for Flurry, he was a very clever bear. He quickly burrowed deep into the box full of Flakey bears, making it very difficult for the toy store workers to find him. One of the workers decided to turn over the box and dump all of the bears out and check each of them one-by-one. "Guard the door, and make sure he doesn't escape," said one of the workers, as the man he spoke to quickly jogged over to the door to secure it.

As careful as the men were to take precautions, Flurry was already making escape plans. He realized that the door handle was too high for him to reach, but he waited patiently for his opportunity. As they combed through the box's contents, it was only a matter of time before they found Flurry.

Then Flurry's moment arrived. It was as if fate had been on his side. Someone opened the door from the other side, and an important-looking female in a gray suit, walked in. "What in the world are you guys doing? Why would you dump all of our merchandise on the floor like that? Are you insane? Pick those bears up right now and put them either in the box or out on the shelves before I decide to fire all three of you!"

The men stumbled over themselves and attempted to give the lady an answer, but they melted before her authoritative demeanor. They picked up the Flakey bears, brushed them off, and placed them back into the box. As she turned around to head back out into the store, Flurry made a run for the door. The men called out, "Get that bear!" but it was too late. Flurry had slipped through the door and into the toy store.

The workers all stood there for a moment, uncertain of what to do. They knew if they didn't pick up the Flakey bears they would be in trouble, but if they could catch Flurry, they would be rich. It didn't take them long to weigh their options and conclude to continue the hunt to catch Flurry. They all quickly ran for the door in hot pursuit.

Flurry ran down the aisles of the toy store, looking for a safe haven. He ran as fast as his little legs would take him. As Flurry was running, a little girl caught sight of him. Her mouth dropped open with awe. She vigorously pulled at her mother's arm, calling to her in earnest, "Mommy! Mommy! Look! Look! That teddy bear's real!"

The little girl's mother looked around and then back down at her. Not seeing anything, her mother answered, "Yes, that's nice, dear," and continued looking at the shelved products.

Luckily for Flurry, nobody else spotted him. This was in part due to his small stature, the fact that he was light on his feet, and that fate had other plans for Flurry. Flurry was very swift on his feet and even swifter with his wit. By keeping his wits about him, he found a way to allude his pursuers.

While thinking to himself about what he should do, he noticed the teddy bear aisle. His face lit up as he said, "I know! I'll hide there. But I'll need a disguise."

Flurry thought for a moment and then darted off to an adjacent aisle looking for scissors and glue. He grabbed the needed tools and then ran to the teddy bear aisle. He didn't waste any time as he hastily cut the tags off one of the teddy bears and glued them to himself. He then hid among the other teddy bears. Normally, he might have stood out a bit, but luckily for Flurry this toy store already had some of his Flakey bears stocked on the shelves.

Flurry held as still as he possibly could,

making sure not to even blink. The men had now started down the aisle in search of him. The leader of the three workers told one of his co-workers, "You, check each and every teddy bear on the shelves here." Pointing at the third member of their team, he continued, "We're going to go check the other aisles." The leader and the other man quickly walked off, leaving only the one worker behind to search through the shelved teddy bears.

The remaining worker was in a hurry and didn't care enough to put any of the bears back on the shelf after checking them. He would just pull one off the shelf, check it, and toss it over his shoulder and onto the floor. Before too long, he had begun amassing a pile of teddy bears on the tiled floor. This worked in Flurry's favor when a security guard came down the aisle and caught the store employee in the act. "Hey! You there! Stop what you're doing and come with me!" said the angry-looking security guard.

"Get lost! Can't you see I'm busy here?" retorted the worker in a defensive tone.

The security guard wasn't amused. He marched over, grabbed the man by the arm and hauled him down the aisle. There they met up with two more security guards, the store manager, and the other two workers who had partnered with the man in their hunt for Flurry.

"I don't know what has gotten into the three of you, but you're all fired! Get out of my store!" the lady barked her orders as she pointed toward the main entrance. The security guards escorted the three men out of the toy store and into the parking lot.

Flurry remained still and decided to continue laying low until nightfall. Flurry thought that if he were to just wait until the store closed, he could slip out and make a phone call to Mr. Kringle, asking him to come pick him up. However, Flurry's plans were thwarted when something even more unexpected happened.

Flurry had been hiding long enough for the employees to brush off and restock the teddy bears, cleaning up the mess the worker had made. Flurry thought that he was safe and in the clear until a man came down the aisle with a shopping cart. The man was very tall and slender. He was probably in his thirties. The pale skinned man had short brown hair, brown eyes, and a goatee. He looked very happy to be in the teddy bear aisle of the store.

Wheeling the cart up in front of the shelf where Flurry sat, the man reached for Flurry, picked him up, and held him in the air. "Wow! This has got to be the cutest teddy bear I have ever seen," the man exclaimed, while examining Flurry from every angle.

Flurry continued to hold still and pretend to be lifeless. The man put Flurry into his cart and headed toward the checkout lane. Flurry was already formulating a new escape plan when the man turned his attention to Flurry again. "My wife has always wanted a teddy bear to add to her collection of plush animals. She'll be so happy when she sees how cute this one is!" the man continued, smiling and petting Flurry's soft white fur.

The man placed Flurry in the hands of the checkout girl. As he did this, she gave Flurry a hug and told the man, "This is the cutest teddy bear I've ever seen! Where did you find him?"

"He was among the other teddy bears in the teddy bear aisle," the man answered.

"I'm going to have to buy one of these for myself," the cashier replied.

"It's a Christmas gift for my wife. She's been looking for just the right teddy bear and I think I have finally found the perfect one," the man explained.

"She's so lucky! Your wife will be so happy when she sees this little guy. I'm assuming it's a boy, with that handsome blue scarf. I'm jealous. I want one too," she said as they both laughed in unison.

The man finished his transaction and exited the building. Flurry was tense. It took every bit of effort to not blink or move. Flurry was already hard at work planning his escape, but he was suddenly placed in the trunk of the car before he even realized what had happened. Trapped! Flurry couldn't do anything until the man reopened the trunk. Realizing this, Flurry impatiently lay there in the dark, feeling frustrated that his plans continued to get foiled time and time again. After all, there he was again, sitting in darkness and unable to escape the locked trunk. "Aw! Will this ever end?" Flurry thought to himself.

Suddenly Flurry felt the wavering of the car's suspension as the gentlemen got inside and turned over the engine. Flurry heard the roar of the engine and soon realized they were on the move. The trunk wasn't the most comfortable of accommodations, and Flurry felt every bump and hole in the road.

The gentleman, however, couldn't be more

happy. He finally found the perfect gift to give to his wife. As he drove along, he thought to himself about how excited his wife would be to see her special gift. He thought about where he would hide the bear, before showing it to his love. His thoughts remained focused on the topic of presenting Flurry to his wife as he drove down the road of the little town named Haengbokville – this little town that he called home.

# Chapter 6
## A LESSON TO LEARN

The gentleman arrived at a lovely looking brick home with a chimney and a big yard. Turning onto a paved driveway, he drove up to the garage that was separate from the house.

Getting out from his car, he quickly and anxiously opened the trunk to get the special gift he had purchased for his wife.

He entered the house to find his wife grading her students' tests – she was an instructor at a university in the nearby metropolis named Miso city.

The couple were very young. They were clearly married, as their matching wedding rings revealed, and the wife looked to be in her mid-twenties – though you can't ever be sure without asking. Not all people look their age, you know. The wife was very beautiful with her long, black hair and thin oriental features. She also wore a pair of black framed glasses, which made her look even more adorable.

It was evident why her husband loved her so much. She had such a sweet and loving quality to her essence.

The gentleman was impatient and wanted to see her face light up at the sight of his Christmas present, but he restrained himself and went into their bedroom to hide the little bear under the bedspread. "There! She won't realize that there's something under her blanket until she gets into bed. Then she'll see the surprise I have waiting for her," the gentleman thought to himself as he left the room and closed the door behind him.

"Finally!" thought Flurry, as he began to put his escape plan into action. "I thought he'd never leave," Flurry muttered to himself as he peeked out from the covers. "What should I do now? I wonder if … ooh!" He caught sight of the young lady's mobile phone, sitting on the nightstand beside him. Flurry's paw shot out from under the bed covering and snagged the phone more quickly than you could blink. Flurry then slipped back under the blanket and began dialing.

The phone number that Flurry dialed

wasn't a typical phone number, as it was a direct line to Christopher Kringle. Flurry was thinking to himself, "Since tonight's Christmas Eve, maybe Santa can swing by and pick me up."

Flurry's phone call was met with much joy. Flurry's mother was the first to pick up the phone. Flurry and his mother shed tears together while they told each other how much they missed and loved each other. Then Flurry spoke with his father and apologized for making them worry, but his father was exceptionally understanding and was relieved to know that his beloved son was safe.

Christopher got on the phone with Flurry and Flurry explained the entire story to him. Flurry went into detail about how all he wanted to do was to look at how cute his

Flakey bears were and how one thing led to another, stranding him in the home of strangers in a strange land named Middleasia.

Flurry wanted to be sure that he got every detail in, but in this case, it worked against him. After hearing what had caused the incident in the first place, Mr. Kringle's countenance changed from compassionate to disciplinary.

Mr. Kringle cleared his throat and his voice became very serious. "Well, young one, that's quite the story," Christopher began. "Seeing as how you got yourself into this mess based upon vanity, I deem it a fitting disciplinary action to leave you there until you can learn humility."

There was a long pause with nothing but silence. Flurry couldn't believe his ears. In fact, Flurry felt outraged that "Santa" would say that. Uncertain of what to say, all Flurry could manage to say was, "But!"

Flurry's short and incomplete response was cut off by Mr. Kringle, as he continued his discourse, "Now, this couple you're staying with, I know of them. They've been unable to have any children, though they very much have longed to have a child of their own. I can speak with confidence that they'll love and cherish you deeply. This punishment is to humble you and teach you to learn that you shouldn't be so stuck on your looks. What's important is what someone's like on the inside, not on the outside. With time all beauty fades, but true beauty, that which is in your deepest parts, is what lasts forever. When you can learn humility and prove to me that you've learned to not be so vain, I'll allow you to return."

Mr. Kringle's decree seemed so harsh and extreme to Flurry. This would mean that he wouldn't get to play with his buddy Sunny or his cousin Bliz. He wouldn't get to have his mama make hot chocolate for him or get to walk to work with his papa. Flurry couldn't hold back the flood ready to burst from his eyes. The tears came flowing like a waterfall. Flurry wept bitterly as he pleaded with Mr. Kringle, "Please Santa! I've learned my lesson. Please let me come back!"

"You may come back for short visits, but you cannot truly return until you've learned the value of inner beauty and shown humility. These are important lessons for raising you up in the ways which are right," Mr. Kringle continued, in an attempt to get Flurry to understand.

"But, what about mama and papa?" Flurry

thought that shifting the focus might convince Christopher of their pain and commute his sentence.

Mr. Kringle could see through Flurry's attempt and reassured Flurry, "I understand what you're saying, and it's true, they'll be sorrowful and miss you. They'll be looked after, and I have something special in mind to ease their pain. They'll also come to visit you from time-to-time, I promise."

Flurry continued to cry. His cries were so loud that there wasn't any reason why the human couple living in the house couldn't or even wouldn't hear him – they were in the next room after all.

Mr. Kringle continued, "Flurry, please allow me to illustrate my lesson with a personal story of my own. Long ago, I had a little pet named Jack. Jack was a red panda and he was the cutest of all red pandas. Now, that's saying a lot, since red pandas are inherently adorable. In many ways, his memory reminds me of you. I came across that little fellow during one of my adventures in the Himalayas. It was one of the worst winters in decades, and I found him close to death and freezing.

Well, I couldn't let any poor animal suffer like that, despite the fact that red pandas are an endangered species. I took him in and saw to his medical needs. He looked as if he had been attacked by another animal.

As time passed, I succeeded in nourishing him back to health. During that time, I had grown quite fond of him. He was like a child to me. In fact, he was my family, before I met my lovely wife.

One day, by the blessing of the king who

gave me the ability to work my miracles, I decided to give little Jack the ability to speak, think, and reason, much like you and me.

It was quite wonderful to be able to teach him new things and to have conversations with him. Over the years we were inseparable. Wherever one was, the other was too. We were the best of friends. I knew I could rely on him for anything. He assisted me and the other teddy bears in building the teddy bear village long, long ago. He acted as my emissary to the warrior elves of the south, who are now the protectors of our land. He was instrumental in befriending the elves. If not for the elves, we wouldn't have our perimeter defense from our enemies and other dangers.

Yet, despite all of our history together, Jack had a darker side that was deep within his heart. It was much like a tiny little mustard seed because it was so small. But time nourished this seed until it grew into something horrible."

"What was that?" Flurry asked him in a deeply concerned voice.

"Well, much like you, everyone adored him. He was loved and praised for his good looks. He was so cute and adorable, how could anyone not love him? At least, that's what he thought. The adoration went to his head, and he began thinking of himself as the cutest of all animals. He went so far as to feel that it was the obligation of all who saw him to compliment him on his cute looks. When someone didn't mention how cute he was, he would become angry inside. He would feel as if he had been wronged.

This anger grew into bitterness and

resentment. He began to have spiteful feelings and ideas of retaliation on those who didn't give him the proper respect and adoration he thought he deserved.

One day, the darkness had grown to full maturity. He decided that enough was enough. So he set out to exact his revenge by stealing all of the Christmas gifts from the homes of those who hadn't told him that he was cute. His vanity destroyed who he was. I lost my best friend and brother to his pride and vanity. And that was only just the beginning of the horrors he brought forth upon our land."

Christopher's voice cracked but he swallowed hard, took a deep breath, and mustered the strength to finish his thoughts. "Flurry, I'm trying to teach you humility, not to be mean or cruel to you. I'm doing this as a means to prevent you from traveling down the path that Jack once took. His heart has grown cold and his thoughts are like frost. Maybe this is why he chose to live in the forbidden land of the ice caves. You're a marvelous little bear, and it would break your mother and father's heart to see you lose your way and your innocence by becoming like Jack. I hope you can understand this."

By bringing the punishment up again, Flurry was reminded of his frustration with Mr. Kringle's decree. Mr. Kringle then finished the phone conversation with his closing statements, "The people you're with are a very loving couple. You'll be deeply appreciated. As for your mother and father here, I'll inform them of my decision and take special care to ensure that they're comforted. I'll be watching over them as well as I'll be watching over you too. You may not be aware of my presence, but I'll be keeping an eye on you. My elves are always watching. So long and farewell little one. Use this time wisely, it could easily be the best time of your life. My best wishes be with you and have a Merry Christmas!"

Flurry felt an overwhelming sense of disappointment. He had been so sure that "Santa" would bring him back home, but Flurry was wrong. Flurry was already missing his parents and friends back at the North Pole.

Flurry began to pout as he realized he was now stuck in this strange land with a couple of strangers. In a moment of rage, Flurry ripped the blanket down from his head, to put the phone back on the nightstand. In the moment of his tantrum he looked up to find the gentleman and his wife standing at the foot of the bed, mouths and eyes wide open.

Still in the midst of his tantrum, Flurry looked at them with a glare and then threw up his arms saying, "What? Haven't you seen a talking teddy bear before?" Then, just as quickly as he threw down the blanket from his head, he grabbed it again, flipped it back up over his head, and continued hiding under the covers.

# Chapter 7
## FLURRY'S NEW LIFE

As time passed, Flurry became like a son to the human couple, and Flurry lovingly called them mommy and daddy. During Flurry's first few weeks in his new home, he did a lot of exploring. He inspected all of the kitchen cabinets, looked under cushions, mattresses, and blankets, and inspected the fireplace as well. He quickly took notice of how he would access certain things, especially food items, now that he was in a home where everything seemed to be giant compared to him. Nothing was his size or within his reach. It was during all of his explorations that he discovered mommy's collection of plush animals. This was the same collection that he was going to be added to originally, when they still believed him to be a regular, inanimate teddy bear.

Among the collection were four little plush animals that caught Flurry's attention. The first two looked like lions, though their appearances vastly differed from each other. One was very tall and slender with a long face and a bushy mane. It had a very interesting gaze, as if it were the wisest among the plush animals. It did look like it had been worn out a bit more than the others, possibly from years of use. Strangely, it also seemed to be without a mouth. Flurry wondered to himself about how that lion would eat, drink, or even talk.

The other lion was very small with a round face and a mane that seemed to stand up as if being held in place by static electricity. Flurry wondered if the little one was a scientist, like Albert Einstein, after noticing his mane being so wild and messy that you couldn't see the little lion's ears, though they must've been there under all of that fur.

The next animal in the lineup was a polar bear. This bear had cream colored fur, black paw pads, and big black, dreamy eyes. It looked like it had been well loved by its keeper.

Last, but not least, Flurry couldn't help but notice how cute the little brown bunny was, though he mistakenly thought it was a mouse at first. As he thought about how cute that little one was, another thought crept into his mind. "He's quite cute, but not as cute as me," Flurry thought to himself. Then Flurry immediately followed up his thought with an "Oops!" when he realized that he was falling into the trap of vanity again.

Being curious about all of them, Flurry attempted to find a way up onto the dresser where they all sat. Unable to find an easier way up, Flurry began to climb. He grunted, huffed, and puffed his way up the dresser until he reached the top. Standing there, he saw many other plush animals that he hadn't seen from his previous vantage point, but he was still interested in the same four that were all lined up in a row next to each other.

"Hello! I'm Flurry!" Flurry called out to them, but they didn't reply or even acknowledge his presence in any way.

Surprised by this, Flurry continued, "What are your names?" Flurry's question was still met with silence. "Oh! You must be playing a game. Okay, I'll play." Flurry sat there in silence for a moment, but like most children, he was unable to sit still for very long.

Flurry jumped back up to his feet and nudged the taller lion on the shoulder, "Do you want to play a game?" The lion still wouldn't answer or even look at him.

Flurry began to feel disappointed and shunned. His new acquaintances didn't seem to have any interest in making a new friend. Flurry was filled with frustration as he crossed his arms and sat down abruptly. In a bit of a tantrum he said, "I wish you guys would talk to me. I just want to be friends." Within that moment, the taller of the two lions turned his head and looked right at

Flurry and waved to him.

Flurry's countenance instantly improved, and he jumped to his feet. "Oh, yeah! You don't have a mouth. No wonder you didn't speak to me," Flurry reasoned out loud. Flurry then walked up to the second lion, the little one, and asked, "What's your name?" That lion answered him saying, "Well, I believe my name is Boaz. That's what my caretakers call me. And him ..." pointing at the taller lion, just over his right shoulder, "His name is Noah, but he won't be able to answer you because he doesn't have a mouth."

"Nice to meet you, Boaz and Noah!" Flurry exclaimed with excitement. Noah waved again.

Before Flurry was done being introduced, the polar bear interjected, "My name's

Caboose!"

"Hi, Caboose! I'm Flurry!"

"Oh! Hi! My name's Caboose!" the polar bear answered.

"Uh … yeah, you already said that," Flurry answered in a tone of uncertainty, as if he were a bit perplexed by Caboose.

"I did? Oh, okay," Caboose replied.

During their interactions, the bunny rabbit kept muttering to himself and looked angry. He began to walk off when suddenly Flurry was standing right in his path. He looked up to see Flurry looking down at him. Flurry reached down and patted the bunny on the head. "You're a cute little mouse. What's your name?"

The bunny pushed Flurry's paws off of his head before turning around and taking off. Speeding away, the little fellow continued muttering something that Flurry couldn't make out.

"His name is Honja. Or at least I think that's his name. That's what our parents call him," Boaz interjected.

"Oh! Hello, Honja! Nice to meet you!" Flurry hollered at him, as Honja hopped toward the other side of the dresser surface.

"Don't mind him. He can be really grumpy. He's probably angry that you thought he was a mouse. He's a bunny rabbit. He doesn't like being patted on the head either," Boaz explained. "Essentially, he's a bit of a loner. He likes to keep to himself."

"Oh! Sorry, Honja!" Flurry called out to the rabbit, hoping to patch up any hard feelings. "Why can't I understand what he is saying?" Flurry asked, turning toward Boaz for the answer.

"Well, our father purchased him in another country. So he doesn't speak our language. Luckily, he seems to be able to understand us," said Boaz.

"Oh! Well, I'm sure I can figure it out. I'm smart!" Flurry assured Boaz. Then Flurry stopped for a moment and thought to himself, "Is that also a vain thought? Oops!"

Now, unbeknownst to Flurry, he was actually responsible for the other four plush animals coming to life. Flurry was unaware that he had any miraculous powers. It wasn't on purpose, but somehow Christopher Kringle's abilities left some residual effects on Flurry after the night he brought Flurry to life. This is how Flurry managed to speed up time when he wanted to go to the toy factory on his first day of work.

Unaware of his miraculous ability, Flurry

had managed to create new friends for himself; though he assumed that these four plush animal dolls had always had the ability to speak and move around just as he did. Flurry was none the wiser that he had anything to do with it.

Needless to say, Flurry's new foster family were in for yet another surprise. The lady of the house was at the computer desk, entering in grades for her students when, out of the corner of her eye, she saw something golden brown standing at the door. She turned to look and found a tall slender lion waving at her. She gasped and jumped up from the chair. "Noah? This isn't possible," she thought to herself.

She carefully walked toward the lion just before he took off running toward the living room area. As she reached the open door of her computer room, she found a bunny rabbit running past her, being closely followed by a polar bear. Hearing a strange sound, she turned around to look back at the computer, only to find the little lion typing away on her keyboard. "Hey! What are you doing?" she exclaimed as she ran over to the computer.

"I'm just looking at the computer, Mommy," little Boaz answered.

Her mouth dropped open, as she tried to take in and understand the events that were unfolding right before her eyes. The house was in a state of chaos as they ran all over the place. Uncertainly she asked, "You can talk?"

"Of course I can!" Boaz said.

"Yeah! Isn't it great, Mommy?" Flurry called to her from the doorway.

"Flurry! How did this happen? How's this

even possible?" she shouted at Flurry.

Thinking he was in trouble, Flurry answered, "Caboose did it! Okay, goodbye!" and tried to run off, but his mommy was quick on her feet, and she grabbed his scarf before he could get away.

Flurry looked back at her, embarrassed. "Flurry!" she said, expecting an account from her little bear.

"What are you talking about, Mommy? These are my friends," Flurry answered, uncertain of why his mommy was so surprised by this.

Not knowing how to answer, she released Flurry and rushed out of the room just as Noah was turning on the television. She had now gotten her senses back and called out to the circus running around her house, "Noah! Boaz! Caboose! Honja! What are all of you doing?" They froze in their tracks and looked up at her.

"Playing?" they answered in a unified voice.

She rubbed her eyes and shook her head. "I can't believe this is happening," she softly whispered to herself. "All of you, come here!" They all ran up to her and lined up in front of her. "Flurry, too!" she added while Flurry was trying to sneak away.

Flurry quickly ran up and got in line, holding his arms behind his back, as he usually did when he was in trouble. "Yes, Mommy?"

"Flurry, did you do this?" she asked.

"Do what?" Flurry asked innocently.

"Bring them to life. Did you do that?" she asked again.

Flurry was quite confused by this and did

the best he could to answer her, "Mommy, they've always been alive. I just went into your room to talk to them, and we all decided to play together."

Their mother sighed and shook her head in disbelief. "How am I going to handle five of them now? Flurry's already a handful as it is," she thought to herself. "Okay, there are some ground rules. Nobody is allowed to watch the television, play video games, or be on the computer without getting my permission first. Nobody is allowed to go outside without me or my husband's supervision – it isn't safe. Stay away from the stove and oven – they're dangerous and you can catch on fire."

They all listened closely as she continued through her rules. When she was finished, they resumed their festivities and played games together.

Later that evening, when her husband pulled into the driveway, she quickly rushed out the front door to debrief him before allowing him to enter the house. She was certain that he would have the same reaction that she previously had … disbelief.

Instead of getting one child, they now had five furry little ones to look after. Their father got different materials together and built beds and nightstands for all of the little ones. He and his wife decided to make the computer room a bedroom for their fuzzy kids.

Flurry was quick to decorate his part of the room by adding a drawing of himself sitting with his new parents. In addition to his drawing was a photograph of himself. He taped them both up on the green wall next to his bed.

To his new parents disapproval, he also wrote his name on the wall in crayon. They were very displeased with Flurry over this, but what was done was done. It wasn't the the last time he would do something like that.

A dresser sat between Flurry and Noah's beds, and they each got one of the drawers to use as their own. The same was done for Caboose, Boaz, and Honja, though Boaz and Honja shared a drawer together.

One morning, Flurry woke up earlier than he normally did. He crawled out of bed and noticed that the other fuzzy animals were still asleep. His mommy was typing away at the computer, hard at work. As the sun shown in through the window, the beams of light illuminated the gray cobblestone design on the floor.

Flurry began to put his bed back in order as he was taught to do. Just as he pulled his blue, snowflake-covered bedspread up over his pillow, he looked around and realized how happy he was with his new family and new life in Middleasia.

Flurry realized that his foster mommy and daddy loved him and cared about him very much. He still got frequent visits from his teddy bear parents. He had new friends and many new and exciting experiences. He thought about how he would never have met such great people or have his new and wonderful friends if he were still at the North Pole. Flurry fondly recalled all of the new food that had been introduced to him, especially his favorites, spaghetti and chocolate milk. Flurry looked around, content, and with a smile on his face he thought to himself, "There's no place like home."

From that day forward, Flurry had many wonderful and exciting experiences. This story is just one of his many adventures.

# ABOUT THE AUTHOR

J.S. Skye and his wife live in their own private castle in the Midwest where they spend their time looking after Flurry, Noah, Caboose, Boaz, and Honja. It's quite a task to keep up with those characters but they manage somehow. J.S. Skye is co-creator of Flurry the Bear, along with his partner J. Leow. J.S. Skye has brought joy into the lives of many through the stories and adventures of Flurry the Bear and friends. Currently, J.S. Skye's hard at work on additional novels in the universe of Flurry the Bear and working on an epic science fiction novel series named *The Seven Seals*. For more information or to get in touch with J.S. Skye personally, he may be contacted by e-mail: contact@js-skye.com

Mr. Snow

Mrs. Snow

**Flurry**

**Sunny**

Mrs. Daybear

Aunt Bubbles

Jinja

Mojo

# Christopher
# Kringle

Jack

**Flurry's Mommy**

**Noah**

**Caboose**

**Honja**
(hōnjä)

**Boaz**
(bōˈăz)

**www.FlurryTheBear.com**

# Flurry teddy bears available by the holiday season of 2012.